"But we still gotta find out how to be like Cupid. We gots to keep from being 'molished!" Tommy declared.

Chuckie sighed and said, "But Tommy, we're running out of time! I'm more worried now! What are we gonna do?"

"Don't you want to be like Cupid in the parade? Don't you want to keep from getting 'molished?" asked Tommy.

"Of course I do," Chuckie replied. "But how?"

Stupid Cupid

Rugrats Chapter Books

Based on the TV series *Rugrats*® created by Arlene Klasky, Gabor Csupo,
and Paul Germain as seen on Nickelodeon®

SIMON SPOTLIGHT
An imprint of Simon & Schuster Children's Publishing Division
1230 Avenue of the Americas, New York, New York 10020

Copyright © 2001 Viacom International Inc.
All rights reserved. NICKELODEON, *Rugrats*, and all related titles, logos,
and characters are trademarks of Viacom International Inc.

All rights reserved including the right of reproduction in whole
or in part in any form.

SIMON SPOTLIGHT and colophon are registered trademarks of
Simon & Schuster.

Manufactured in the United States of America

First Edition

2 4 6 8 10 9 7 5 3 1

ISBN 0-689-83819-0

Library of Congress Control Number 00-133514

Stupid Cupid

by Nancy Krulik
illustrated by Carlos Ortega

Simon Spotlight/Nickelodeon

New York   London   Toronto   Sydney   Singapore

Chapter 1

"Tommy, what's Valumtime's Day?" Chuckie Finster asked his best friend, Tommy Pickles. They were in a greeting card and party goods store.

"I'm not sure," Tommy whispered. "It's got something to do with hearts, I think. And it also has something to do with cookies. My mom's been baking them all week. They smell really yummy!"

"I think I'm gonna like Valumtime's Day," Chuckie said with a smile.

The boys' conversation was cut short by Stu, Tommy's dad, who held up a Valentine's Day card for Tommy to see. "What do you think of this one, sport?" asked Stu.

Tommy looked at the bright red greeting card his father had in his hand. The valentine had a picture on it of a baby in a diaper holding a bow and arrow. Tommy grinned. He loved looking at pictures of other babies.

"I like that one too," Stu said to Tommy. "I've always had a soft spot for Cupid. He makes the whole world fall in love."

As the two boys sat side by side in their strollers, Stu and Chas, Chuckie's dad, searched shelf after shelf of

Valentine's Day cards. Stu was trying to find just the right one to give to Tommy's mom, Didi. Chas was looking for a valentine for Kira, who was his new wife and Chuckie's new mom.

"Here are some good ones for you, Stu," Chas said as he handed Stu several cards.

Stu opened the first card and read, "'I've flipped for you!'" It had a picture of Cupid upside down doing a handstand on the front. "Well, I don't know, Chas."

"That's all right," replied Chas. "I'll give that one to Kira. How about one of the other cards?"

Stu said, "This one says, 'I've got a case of puppy love.' Oh no, this isn't right, either."

"Well, what about the last card I

gave you?" Chas reminded Stu.

"This card says, 'I am filled with love for you.' It has hearts and a rose. That's more Didi's style. This is the one!" Stu declared.

Stu and Chas went to the cash register. As the clerk rang up the sale, Stu noticed a sign on the counter.

"'Enter your child in the Cutie Cupid Contest,'" he read. "'Have your child play Cupid and ride on top of the heart float in our annual Valentine's Day Parade,'" Stu read on. "'Judging will take place on Valentine's Day.'"

Stu looked down at Tommy in his stroller. He had to admit that Tommy was really cute. Maybe he could win. "Chas, I'm entering Tommy in this Cutie Cupid Contest."

"What a good idea!" Chas exclaimed.

"I think I'll enter Chuckie, too."

Just then another father walked over to the counter. He was very tall and had some very big muscles. His baby son was sitting in a stroller beside Tommy and Chuckie. "Your babies don't stand a chance against my Sammy here," the huge father told them. "Sammy's a natural for playing Cupid. Look at his gorgeous blond curls. And Sammy's a professional actor. You must have seen him on the Reptar commercials."

"*That's* where I know that baby from," Tommy whispered to Chuckie. "He's a friend of Reptar's. I saw them together on TV."

Chuckie smiled at Sammy. Sammy yawned.

Stu looked up at the muscular father

and tried to speak. "We'll see," he mumbled. "My Tommy is pretty cute too, you know."

"And so is my Chuckie," Chas added, suddenly feeling braver. "A kid doesn't have to be on TV to be lovable."

The big dad let out a thunderous laugh. "Go ahead and enter, if you want. But *my* kid's gonna be Cupid, and we're gonna demolish you guys in that contest!"

And with that, Sammy and his dad left the card shop, leaving Stu and Chas to fill out their entry forms. As they were leaving, Sammy stuck his tongue out at Chuckie and Tommy.

"Did you hear what that daddy said, Tommy?" Chuckie whispered. "They're gonna 'molish us!"

"What does 'molish mean?" Tommy asked.

"I don't know," Chuckie admitted. "But it sure sounds bad!"

"Maybe," Tommy said, "we just gots to be Cupids too. Then we won't get 'molished!"

Chapter 2

When Valentine's Day arrived the next day, everyone in the Pickles house was excited. Stu had just put the finishing touches on a special Valentine's Day project. Baby Dil was all dressed up in red, and Tommy was trying to put together a heart-shaped puzzle. Didi was baking heart-shaped cookies, and Grandpa Lou was in the kitchen munching on one of those cookies.

"Mmm! Mmm! I love these cookies, Didi!" Grandpa Lou exclaimed.

"Thanks, Pop!" replied Didi. "You know what they say: 'Love is what makes the world go around!'"

"I know Cupid sure made the earth move for me," Stu said, coming into the kitchen and giving Didi a hug. "Everybody needs love."

Dingdong!

Just then the doorbell rang. It was Chuckie and Chas.

"Hey there, Chas," Stu said as he opened the front door. "I'm glad you got here early. There's something I want to show you in my workshop."

Chuckie sighed as he watched Chas and Stu disappear down the basement stairs.

"What's the matter, Chuckie?" Tommy asked.

"I'm still worried about this Cupid Contest, Tommy," Chuckie replied. "I don't want my daddy to be 'molished, but I don't think I have what it takes to be a Cupid."

"Why not, Chuckie?"

"'Cuz I have red hair, and I wear glasses. And I don't wear diapers anymore. I'm not anything like Cupid."

Tommy shrugged. "But that's just what Cupid *looks* like. We don't know what kind of kid he is. Maybe you're a lot like him."

"What kind of baby do you think Cupid is?" Chuckie asked.

"Well, it's his job to make people fall in love, and there's only one of him and lots of people to get to fall in love. So I'll bet that means he's real strong," Tommy mused. "He's gotta be strong to shoot his love arrows too. My daddy said that Cupid made the earth move. So maybe Cupid makes people fall in love by moving the world around?"

Chuckie thought about that for a while. "Yeah. If the world starts moving around, people might fall into each other's arms. Just like hugging."

"That's why I think Cupid must be a *really* strong baby. And if we want to be Cupids in the parade, we gots to be just like him," Tommy agreed.

Chuckie tried to make a muscle. "I don't think I'd make a good Cupid, then, Tommy," Chuckie admitted. "I'm not real strong."

"I'm not, either," Tommy assured him. "At least not yet. But I will be."

Chuckie looked confused.

"My mommy goes to the gym to get muscles. Sometimes she takes me with her," Tommy explained. "We could do the kind of stuff she does there. See, watch."

He toddled over to where his father had dropped Tommy's coat, hat, and mittens in a pile on the floor. Carefully, he put on his mittens. Then he toddled over to his blowup clown and gave it a good punch. It wobbled back and forth and finally righted itself. Tommy punched the clown again. He was pretending to be a big, strong boxer.

"Well, that's okay for you," Chuckie said. "But I *hate* clowns. They're too scary." Chuckie sat on the floor and looked at his shoes with disappointment. "I guess I'll *never* be Cupid in that parade."

Tommy stopped boxing the clown balloon and went to comfort his friend. "Sure you will, Chuckie," he said. "Just follow me."

Tommy toddled over to the staircase and started climbing his way upstairs. "At my mommy's gym they have this machine that moves up and down when you stand on it. It's kind of like walking on stairs 'cept you don't go anywhere. We could climb our stairs. And that's even better 'cuz we'll get somewhere—upstairs."

Chuckie brightened. Climbing the stairs didn't seem too scary. It even sounded sort of fun. He followed Tommy to the stairs at the front hall.

"Okay, here we go," Tommy said. He got on all fours and climbed up the first two steps. Chuckie followed close behind.

By the time the babies had reached the fourth step, Didi came around the bend. She spotted Chuckie and Tommy and ran up behind them. "What are you two doing here?" she asked calmly. "You know you're not allowed on the stairs."

Quickly, she scooped up the babies and placed them in their playpen. "Tommy, why are you still wearing your mittens?" she asked as she pulled them off. "I have a lot of work to do for Valentine's Day. So you two play in the playpen for now."

As Didi left the room, Chuckie looked toward Tommy. "Now what are we going to do?" he asked. "There's no way we're going to get strong enough to make the world go around if we're stuck in here."

Tommy grinned. Since when were the babies ever stuck where the growed-ups put them?

Chapter 3

Tommy reached into his diaper and pulled out his screwdriver. He expertly used it to force open the latch on his playpen.

Once he was free, Tommy walked over to the couch. Carefully he pulled down two throw pillows. Then he spread his legs really wide, put his hands flat on the floor, rested his head on one of the pillows, and tried lifting

his legs off the ground. Tommy was trying to stand on his hands, but his little legs wouldn't let him.

Chuckie stared with concern. Obviously all that worrying about getting 'molished had finally gotten to Tommy. Why else would he be looking at the whole world from upside down?

"Remember that card where Cupid was upside down?" asked Tommy. "Maybe Cupid walks around like this."

Chuckie scratched his head. He'd never seen anyone walking around all bent over upside down. Still, Tommy's idea was the only one the two babies had. And the contest was this afternoon! So Chuckie tried to turn himself upside down as well.

Ping!

As his head went down, Chuckie's

glasses fell off of his face and landed on the floor. The room started to look really blurry to him. Then, as if that weren't bad enough, the blood rushed to his head and his cheeks began to feel really hot.

"Hey, Chuckie, you're starting to look more like Cupid already!" Tommy told his friend.

"I am?" Chuckie asked excitedly. "How?"

"Your face. It's turning all red. That's the color of love," explained Tommy.

"Tommy, do you think Cupid feels really dizzy when he makes people fall in love?" Chuckie asked just before he fell backward onto the floor.

Smash!

Uh-oh. Chuckie landed right on top of his glasses.

"Oh no! Now what am I gonna do?" Chuckie moaned as he felt around for his broken glasses.

Tommy picked up Chuckie's glasses. They weren't too badly broken. Luckily Chuckie had landed on the earpiece instead of the lenses.

"They're okay," Tommy assured him.

Chuckie put his glasses back on. One side hung lower than the other, and the nosepiece was a little cracked, but at least he could see.

"We don't have any better chance of becoming Cupid than Dil does," Chuckie said sadly.

Tommy looked over at his baby brother. He could barely hold his own bottle. How could *he* make people fall in love the way Cupid did?

"Don't say that, Chuckie!" Tommy

insisted. "There's still plenty of ways that we can be more like Cupid."

Chuckie looked outside. It had started to rain. Suddenly, the boys heard a loud, frantic scratching at the door. It was Spike trying to come inside!

Tommy's eyes widened at the sound. "That's it!" he exclaimed.

Chapter 4

Quickly Tommy toddled over to the front door. "Chuckie, do you remember when my daddy was talking about puppy love?" Tommy asked. "Well, what if Cupid kisses a puppy, and then that gives him a special power to make people fall in love? It's Puppy Love Power!"

"So are you saying we gots to kiss Spike?" Chuckie asked.

"Chuckie, a baby's gotta do what a baby's gotta do!" Tommy declared.

Chuckie walked over and crouched down beside Tommy. Tommy climbed up on his friend's back and turned the doorknob on the front door. The door swung open, and Spike raced inside.

Spike stood in the doorway and shook the rainwater from his coat. Yucky, muddy water flew in all directions.

"I don't know about this, Tommy," Chuckie murmured, ducking out of the way of one of the black, muddy raindrops. Chuckie sniffed at the air. "Spike stinks!" he exclaimed.

Tommy turned toward Spike, held his nose, puckered up his lips, and kissed Spike right on his wet, black nose.

Spike barked in surprise. He leaped

up in the air and ran off. Chuckie was in his path, but the dog just kept running. He knocked Chuckie to the ground, covering him head to toe in wet, smelly mud.

Spike ran toward the kitchen. Suddenly the boys heard a loud crashing noise. "Spike! Where did you come from?" Didi cried out. "How did you get so dirty?"

Chuckie and Tommy wandered into the kitchen. There they discovered Spike surrounded by a dozen hot, heart-shaped cookies. Didi had been just setting them out to cool when Spike plowed into her.

Quickly she picked up the fallen cookies from the floor to make sure Spike didn't eat any of them. "Oh well." She sighed. "I can always bake more."

When she was finished, she turned her attention to Chuckie and Tommy. "Just look at you two! You're covered in mud too!" she exclaimed. "I guess it's bath time."

Didi scooped Tommy up in her arms and grabbed for Chuckie's hand. Looks like I'll have to get your emergency replacement pair of glasses, Chuckie," Didi added. Then she took the two boys upstairs to the bathroom.

A few minutes later when Tommy and Chuckie were sitting in a big bubble bath, Chuckie asked the question he'd been bursting to ask, "Do you feel Puppy Love Power, Tommy?"

Tommy sat for a moment and waited. But he didn't feel anything.

"No! Nothing happened! Kissing

Spike didn't give me any power," he admitted finally.

"But you got to take a bubble bath, Tommy," Chuckie replied. "And that's fun! I *love* bubble baths."

Tommy smiled. He picked up a bubble in his hand and blew it in the air. "Yeah, Chuckie. Me too," he agreed. "But we still gotta find out how to be like Cupid. We gots to keep from being 'molished!" Tommy declared.

Chuckie sighed and said, "But Tommy, we're running out of time! I'm more worried now! What are we gonna do?"

"Don't you want to be like Cupid in the parade? Don't you want to keep from getting 'molished?" asked Tommy.

"Of course I do," Chuckie replied. "But how?"

Chapter 5

Dingdong!

Tommy and Chuckie were already cleaned up and dressed for the contest when the doorbell rang. Didi opened the door. It was Betty, with Phil and Lil in tow.

"Deed, you mind watching the twins for a few minutes?" Betty asked. "I've got to take my morning run."

"Sure, Betty!" Didi said.

Didi put the twins in the playpen with Tommy and Chuckie.

"Be good!" Didi told them. "Oh, I hear Dil crying! He must be up from his nap. I'll be right back!"

Phil looked curiously at Tommy and Chuckie. He knew something was up. "What're you guys doing?" he asked. "We're trying to become Cupid," Tommy explained.

"But it doesn't seem to be working," Chuckie added. "We're not strong enough, we get dizzy standing on our heads, and kissing Spike doesn't give us any Puppy Love Power at all."

Lil's eyes opened wide with excitement. "Wow! You kissed a dog?" she asked.

Chuckie pointed at Tommy. "He did."
Phil and Lil moved closer to Tommy.

"Why do you want to be someone named Cupid?" Phil asked.

"If you get picked to be Cupid, you get to ride on a big float in a parade at the mall. Our daddies entered us in the contest," Tommy explained.

"And we really have to win. Otherwise this great big daddy will 'molish us," Chuckie continued. "And he could do it too. 'Specially 'cause his baby is Reptar's best friend!"

"Uh-oh. You're in big troubles," said Lil. "*Nobody* can beat Reptar!"

"What are we gonna do?" Chuckie sighed nervously.

Phil sniffed in the air and said, "Mmm. I smell cookies. Maybe we could think better if our tummies were full."

Tommy and Chuckie couldn't argue with that logic. They loved cookies.

Tommy pulled his screwdriver out of his diaper and undid the latch on the playpen. Then he led his friends into the kitchen. Everywhere they looked they could see stacks of heart-shaped cookies. The ones on the counter were sprinkled with pink sugar. The ones on the table had white icing. The ones on top of the stove were shaped like small hearts with icing-covered arrows through them.

Tommy's eyes brightened. "I think I know how we can become Cupid, Chuckie!" Tommy announced excitedly. "We have to eat lots and lots of cookies!"

"That sounds good," Chuckie agreed. He picked up an iced cookie. He was just about to pop it into his mouth when he stopped and asked, "How will eating cookies turn us into Cupid?"

"If you're gonna be Cupid, you gotta be filled with love," Tommy replied. "And hearts mean love, right? So you gotta fill yourself up with these heart cookies!"

Tommy and Chuckie didn't know if this plan would work or not. But they sure wanted to try some of the cookies. So they each popped one into their mouths.

"Now eat lots and lots of them, Chuckie," Lil ordered them as she and Phil grabbed some cookies and stuffed their mouths. Chuckie didn't have to be told twice. The sweet, chewy cookies were so delicious, he could have eaten every single one of them. Obviously, Tommy felt the same way.

He was shoveling heart-shaped cookies into his mouth two at a time.

By the time Chuckie had eaten his fifth cookie, his stomach started to feel funny. "Uh . . . guys . . . I don't feel so good," Chuckie said uneasily.

Tommy nodded and rubbed his own belly. "I don't, either," he confessed as he put down the cookie he held in his hand. "Oooo."

"If this is what it feels like to be full of love all the time, I don't think I want to be Cupid anymore," Chuckie moaned. "Love hurts!"

Chuckie crawled down from his chair and walked slowly into the living room. For the first time in his life, he didn't want to see any more cookies. The other babies followed close behind.

Just then Stu and Chas came upstairs from the basement.

"Well, Tommy and Chuckie, it's time to go to the mall for the Valentine's Day Parade," Stu announced. He smiled at the boys.

"I'll bet one of you is going to win the Cupid Contest," Chas chimed in. "You're going to make us so proud!"

"Hey, Deed!" Stu called. "Chas and I are going out to warm up the car!"

"I'll be right down, dear," Didi replied.

Right after Stu and Chas left the living room, Didi came down the stairs. She was carrying Dil. "Tommy, I'll bet you and Chuckie are very excited! We'll be leaving in just a few minutes." Didi put Dil in his infant seat. Then she went upstairs to finish getting ready.

Chuckie turned to Dil and frowned.

"You are so lucky to be little," he whispered. "Nobody 'spects you to turn into Cupid."

Dil pulled the bottle from his mouth and smiled brightly.

"You know what, Tommy," Chuckie announced. "I don't think I want to be the real Cupid anymore. If he's the kind of baby who stands on his head till he gets dizzy, kisses smelly dogs, and eats too many cookies, then I think Cupid is stupid."

"Stupid Cupid," Lil agreed. "Who wants to be in a parade, anyway?"

"Yeah! Stupid Cupid!" Phil exclaimed. "I'm glad our mommy doesn't want us to be Cupid!"

"Stupid Cupid. Stupid Cupid," Phil and Lil began marching around the room, chanting.

Tommy and Chuckie looked at each other. Cupid might be stupid, but they knew they would be in real trouble if one of them didn't get picked to be Cupid in the parade.

Chapter 6

By the time they all got to the mall, it was very crowded. Chas's wife, Kira, and their daughter, Kimi, were already there waiting for them. Hundreds of parents had come with their babies. Each one was convinced that their child had what it took to be Cupid in the parade.

Chuckie looked at the big heart-shaped float and yawned. It was warm in the mall. And it was late in the day. Didi had been so busy baking cookies that she had forgotten to put Tommy and Chuckie down for their naps. Tommy saw Chuckie open his mouth to yawn, and then he yawned too. Yawning was catching—kind of like the chicken pops he'd had last spring.

The judges began walking through the crowd. They went up and down the line of children, looking at each one, and making notes on their clipboards. Finally the judges stopped in front of Chuckie.

"Chuckie, smile for the nice judges," Chas urged his son.

But Chuckie didn't smile. He just let out a loud zzzzzzz. Chuckie was fast asleep in his stroller.

Kira looked down at Chuckie as the judge walked away. "Sorry about that, Chas," Kira said. "I guess Chuckie won't be Cupid today."

Chas shrugged. "I don't think Tommy's gonna make it, either, Stu," he remarked.

Stu looked down at Tommy's stroller and said to Didi, "Aw, Tommy's already asleep too!"

"Well, I guess these two babies are too pooped to be in the parade," one of the judges remarked as he made his way down the line after the first judge.

Just then Dil's pacifier popped right out of his mouth and fell on the floor. Dil didn't like being without his pacifier. But he was stuck in the baby carrier Didi was wearing.

Frantically Dil kicked his little legs, trying to get someone's attention. And he kicked one of the judges right in the stomach!

The judge smiled at Didi and Stu and asked, "Who is *this* little fellow?" as he bent down to pick up Dil's pacifier and hand it back to Didi.

"That's our younger son, Dil Pickles," Stu answered.

"Gentlemen!" the judge called to the other judges who were still walking up and down the long line of children. "I think I've found our Cupid!" he announced. "Dil Pickles will ride atop our Valentine's Day float in just one hour!"

One hour later a deep voice blasted over the mall loudspeaker system,

"Ladies and gentlemen, welcome to our annual Valentine's Day Parade!" Music began playing loudly throughout the mall. The whole building shook with excitement.

The noise woke Tommy and Chuckie. When they opened their eyes they saw the parade had already begun. There were clowns holding big heart-shaped balloons. Acrobats, dressed as Valentine's Day cards, did flips as they passed by the crowd. Chuckie looked to his left. There was the big, heart-shaped float they had heard so much about. And sitting on top of the float was . . .

"Dil?" Tommy wondered aloud.

"Chuckie! Tommy! Hey, wake up!" Kimi whispered. She tugged on each of their sleeves.

"Wow!" Chuckie whispered. "He didn't have to kiss a puppy or stand on his head or anything."

"I wonder how he did it," said Tommy.

Just then Sammy and his really big dad walked by. It was obvious that Sammy's dad did not want Stu and Chas to notice him. But it's hard to miss a big, tall, muscular man who is crying into his handkerchief.

"Hey, sorry your son didn't get to be Cupid," Stu said to him. "Did you hear? My son was the winner."

The man looked strangely at Stu. "How can that be?" Sammy's dad asked. "Your kid's right there."

Chas grinned and explained, "His *other* son, Dil, won the contest."

Stu nodded and remarked, "Pretty

amazing, huh? Especially since he's not even a professional actor from the Reptar commercials or anything."

Sammy's dad slumped at the shoulders. Suddenly he didn't look so big and scary anymore.

Tommy and Chuckie smiled. They weren't going to be 'molished after all. Dil had saved the day!

"Well, Chuckie!" Chas exclaimed as he bent down and gave Chuckie a kiss. "You may not be Cupid in the parade, but you sure are Cupid to me. You've brought lots of love into my life! You too, Kira and Kimi!"

Stu and Didi smiled at Tommy. "You too, sport," Stu agreed. "You and Dil are our two Cupids."

"That means our house is full of twice the love all year round," Didi

added as she hugged Tommy and Dil.

Tommy and Chuckie looked at each other and grinned. Maybe Cupid wasn't so stupid after all.

About the Author

Nancy Krulik is the author of more than one hundred books for children and young adults, including several based on the Nickelodeon TV series *Rugrats* and *CatDog*. She's also written for several Nick Jr. TV shows, including *Eureeka's Castle* and *Gullah Gullah Island*.

Nancy lives in Manhattan with her husband Danny and their two children, so she feels like Cupid's arrow has struck her three times. Nancy's favorite thing about Valentine's Day is that her husband always gives her lots of chocolates. YUM!